OPHELIA

VICKI-ANN BUSH

For mom, thank you for every moment you listened when I was hurting. Every time I needed advice, whether I asked or not, it was always right. For your Reader's Digest medical opinion, once again, usually right. And for all the laughs, hugs, and love you gave me through the years. I miss you more than words could ever describe, until we meet again, I'll keep listening.

Edited by Celeste Hawkins, Antonia Silic, & Cindy Kilbourne

Original cover & interior design by Shayne Leighton

New Cover Design by Dark Angel Graphics

1

THE BREATHER

S itting in the Grand Hall for assembly, Ophelia nervously scanned the aisles for her friends. Unlike them, she was the least confident of the group. They had met in the ninth grade and clicked instantly. Once she let a layer of her guard down, with a little coaxing, a strong bond was forged.

The Grand Hall reminded Ophelia of Radio City Music hall in N.Y. with its red brocade drapes pulled back with large gold tassels which framed the stage and drew the viewer's eye to one of the many rich patterns throughout a masterpiece of design. A warm glow emanating from gas-fueled sconces reflected the black and gold Victorian scroll wallpaper. Over-sized seats, cushioned velvet and stuffed for supreme comfort, filled both levels accommodating the entire student body and staff.

Amry was the first to induct her into what would become their inner circle. She was so different than Ophelia. Amry was fearless. Beautiful, confident, and the desire for most of the boys. She reminded Ophelia of a painting her mother loved, *Goddess of Summer*. A strong jawline framed the gentle curves of Amry's apple cheeks. Long lashes fringed above the greenest eyes Ophelia had ever seen, and her chestnut locks cascaded to the middle of her back. But her outward appearance was only enhanced by her inner beauty. Amry was not a cliché.

Ophelia spotted her gliding down the hall, two aisles over.

"Amry!" Ophelia flailed her arms.

Spinning to find the direction of her friend's voice, Amry smiled when she spotted two pale arms waving above the crowd's heads.

"Hey, where's everybody?" Amry settled in her seat.

"I don't know but if they're not here soon Dictator Dick will write them up and Kyle can't afford any more negatives." Ophelia frowned.

Amry slumped down in her seat, twirling the ends of her chestnut hair around her finger.

"How did he get that name anyway?"

"Richard Cander. Richard... Dick, and he's a power jerk. Dictator Dick," Ophelia grinned.

"You're always so polite Ophelia," Amry nudge her.

"What do you mean?" Ophelia's eye widened.

"He's a power jerk? Everyone knows he's a mean bastard."

"I don't know," Ophelia paused. "'Bastard' is a strong word. I think he's trying to keep us safe and sometimes it comes off like he's nasty or doesn't care. But I think it's the opposite."

"Our little Ophelia, always seeing the good. That's what I love about you, Lia."

Amry tilted her head to touch Ophelia's.

"You're right. He probably has our safety in mind, but he could go about it another way. Say it with a little kindness."

"That's just it, though. If he did, chances are he'd have a

harder time getting everyone to listen. This way they may not like him, but he gets the job done." Ophelia frowned.

"Potato, patato. Either way, Kyle's ass is grass if he's not here in the next two minutes."

"Whose ass is grass?" At that moment Kyle plopped down in the seat next to Amry. "And why would anyone want an ass made out of grass?"

"There you are," said Amry. "Dictator Dick is getting ready to start, and you almost missed opening pledge. You're already skating on thin ice with him. One more, Kyle and..."

"I know, I know. My ass is grass." Kyle smirked.

"Hey, what'd I miss?" Bethany slid in next to him.

"Nothing much. We were just discussing the botanical growth on my ass."

"What?" Bethany's brows furrowed.

"Never mind. He's just being an idiot," Amry shook her head.

The lights flickered twice indicating it was time for silence. Mr. Abernathy, the Headmaster and school creator, appeared on stage in his usual grand entrance. A man for the dramatic flair, smoke billowed around him while blue and green spotlights circled his frame; all of it a contradiction to his plain black suit. Standing center stage, he cleared his throat. The raspy sound resonated into the microphone and carried throughout the enormous room.

"Attention! Attention everyone! Nice to see you are all looking fine today, and on time, Mr. Burkletter," Abernathy eyeballed Kyle.

"I wonder why those other men are on stage with him," Ophelia whispered.

"Why and who? They're like the Secret Service only not." Amry squinted.

"You having trouble seeing?"

"Yeah. It's okay. I'm not so sure I want to," said Amry chuckling.

"What do you mean?" Ophelia leaned in closer.

"Check it out, Lia. Notice they're wearing khakis and golf shirts. I mean, on all the occasions they came here attached to some political parody, did they ever wear anything other than a dark suit?"

"You have a point."

"They're not radioed up," Amry continued. "Look at their ears, no buds. But they're scouring the surroundings like they're military. I guess we're about to find out."

Mr. Abernathy motioned for the two gentlemen to move forward. They settled on either side of the Headmaster.

"I'd like to introduce Mr. Coal and Mr. Rain. You will be seeing them monitoring the halls for the next few weeks." The headmaster nodded to the two men. "Pay no attention to them and continue to go about your normal, daily business. They will do their best not to interfere with you either."

Stepping back from center stage, he took a moment of silence to wait for the low rumbling of comments to dissipate.

"Now, this brings me to the nature of our assembly today. I need all of you to pay attention to what I'm about to tell you. I need you to understand this is told in the strictest of confidence. You are not to utter one word to anyone."

"Okay, he's starting to scare me," Ophelia shivered.

"Chill, let's hear what the man's gotta say," said Amry.

Ophelia glanced at her friend from the corner of her eye. Amry was the textbook definition of calm, she took things as they came. Ophelia wanted to be more like that, but she was born with a very different kind of psyche. Hers would be right next to the word, anxiety.

There was a low buzz of voices echoing through the room.

"Quiet, please." Mr. Abernathy said, bringing everyone's attention back to him. "A new student will be joining us tomorrow. His name is Sawyer Thomas and I want all of you to make him feel welcome.

He is a bit—different than you, and I wouldn't want that to stop any of you from being friendly. The circumstances that bring him to us are sensitive and, for Sawyer, dire. When I ask you for complete cooperation and discretion, I expect it. You could cost this boy more than you know," His tone changed as the speech took a sinister turn.

"I will be assigning a group of you to accompany Sawyer and give him the full tour of the school. I expect you will do everything you can to make him feel comfortable and welcome at the Academy," he turned and looked at Ophelia and her friends. "Miss Ophelia Wetherton, Miss Amry Goodman, Miss Bethany Smithson, and of course, Mr. Kyle Burkletter, I would like all of you to meet me in my office promptly." He paused for a moment. "That is all for now, you may go back to class," With that Mr. Abernathy glided off stage.

Ophelia sat, unable to move. She wiped the moisture off her palms on the sides of her pants. Struggling to swallow past the lump in her throat, she began taking quick shallow breaths.

"Lia, you okay?" Amry rubbed her back.

Ophelia closed her eyes and concentrated on the reality of her situation. Slowing her breathing to a normal pace.

"Damn. I still can't figure out how you do that," Kyle stood up.

"Stop it Kyle, you'll only make it worse," Bethany grabbed his hand and tugged him forward.

"What did I say?"

"Never mind. Come on, let's go," She led him toward the doors.

"You guys go on ahead. We'll be there in a minute," Amry smiled.

Ophelia knew why Kyle was confused. *She* was confused. It never made any sense to her how anxiety could still overwhelm her. And the breathing, she couldn't even begin to understand where that came from.

"Hey, are you ready to roll? I don't want Abernathy getting on our case," Said Amry, jumping up.

"Yeah. Come on, let's go." As they made their way Ophelia couldn't help but wonder, who was this boy?

The Headmaster's office was a close second to the Grand Hall when it came to luxury. A century old, mahogany desk was the focal point of the room. Mr. Abernathy was seated, hands folded, and posture erect.

Mr. Coal and Mr. Rain were on the left side of the room, each sat on a yellow and blue, floral, wingback chair. They were as stiff in the office as they had been on stage. Dictator Dick was a different story. His grin was so wide, the Cheshire cat would be jealous. He took up space in a small chair to the right.

"Come in, children. Sit, please." He motioned toward a plush four cushion couch with light blue, paisley print in front of his desk.

Ophelia trembled. She hated confrontation of any kind. She sandwiched herself in between Amry and Bethany. The friend blanket was comforting.

"I'm sure you're wondering why I called you here," Abernathy began. "I've chosen your band of outlaws to be hosts to our guest. As I said, Sawyer Thomas will arrive tomorrow, sometime around noon."

"Why us? We're not exactly the cheerleading squad," said Kyle, leaning forward.

"That's exactly why I chose you. I feel confident that being with your group will keep his anonymity."

"So, we're the rejects now?" Kyle's tone was snarky.

"No, Mr. Burkletter quite the contrary. It's your friendship that leads me to believe he will have his best chance at getting through this if he is with you. You watch out for each other, protect one another. I'm asking you to do the same for him."

Ophelia looked over at Amry who was frowning.

"Mr. Abernathy?" Ophelia timidly raised her hand.

"Ophelia my dear, this isn't a classroom. Put your hand down and speak."

"What has this boy done?"

"Done?" Mr. Abernathy raised a brow.

"To bring him here? You said he needed protection. Has he done something to anger the council?" Ophelia spoke in small voice.

"The council? No. I'm afraid Sawyer's issue are much bigger than the council."

Ophelia shuddered. Bigger than the council? What could be worse than having to deal with them?

"I don't understand, Headmaster."

"I don't think any of us do, Lia." Amry stood up. "What is going on?"

"Tone, Miss Goodman." Mr. Abernathy huffed. "This is a delicate matter that will need your-"

"Stop. Just tell us." Amry folded her arms.

"Quit taking the long way around." Kyle said, firmly.

"Sawyer, Mr. Thomas, is a breather."

The four gasped. Ophelia locked eyes with Amry as she slid back into her space on the couch and the room fell silent.

Mr. Abernathy nodded at Dictator Dick. He turned to an oversized étagère on the wall behind him and opened the perfectly crafted doors to reveal six drawers. Sliding open the top one, he pulled out a manila folder and placed it on the desk in front of the teens.

"Open it." Mr. Abernathy nodded his head.

Amry reached out and flipped the folder revealing a black and white photo followed by several sheets of paper.

"All your questions can be answered in this file. We will give you a few minutes to review it and then the rest is up to you. I expect you will treat this boy with the same dignity you would want for yourselves. Regardless if he is a breather or not, he is in danger and I promised safety within these walls."

After the four men left the room, the group huddled together reading the contents of the file.

Ophelia snatched the picture and studied it. A twinge of exhilaration wrapped itself around her petite frame and squeezed. She smiled.

"What the hell are you grinning about?" Ophelia hadn't noticed Kyle's stare.

"Nothing. I was just wondering what he's like." Ophelia dropped the photo on the desk.

"We're all damned." Kyle scowled.

"He's right. We're screwed." Bethany slouched down in the seat.

"We don't have a choice." Amry read the pages again.

"The headmaster picked us for a reason. I'm not happy about this either, but maybe we're this Sawyer's best chance." Ophelia glanced at the photo again. "He's probably really scared. I would be. What's the harm in helping him?"

"Oh, no. He's not even here yet and already she's got them going to the prom," Kyle said, sarcastically.

Ophelia turned away.

"Stop. All of you. Kyle, shut up. Lia, turn back around and Bethany, control your boyfriend," it was apparent that Amry had had enough because she continued. "We don't have a choice. We may not like it but that is how it is. This guy is going to be freaked out enough, imagine when he gets here. Cut him some slack, you read the file. None of this is his fault. We do our best to help him, end of story. Agreed?' Amry tapped her fingers on the desk. "I said, agreed?"

Kyle and Bethany mumbled a reluctant agreement and Ophelia softly smiled.

"Okay then, I'll go tell them we're ready for tomorrow."

Ophelia took one last long gaze at Sawyer's photo before closing the file. There was that twinge again.

2

SAWYER'S FIRST DAY

Ophelia barely slept that night; the anticipation of their new ward left her with too many questions to count. Sawyer was due to embark on his secretive journey of one of the Academy's newest inductees in about an hour, and she was on edge. The fact that he was a breather confused her the most. How could he come to this school? It made no sense.

A harsh thump on her dorm room window startled Ophelia into the now. Turning toward the window she saw a barrage of small stones hit the glass. Frowning, she quickly walked over to see who the pitcher was.

Releasing the latch, she pulled up the window just as another handful of stones sailed toward her face, hitting her square between the eyes at the bridge of her nose.

"Ouch. What the hell, Kyle?" Ophelia tried to rub away the pain.

"Sorry. I guess I should have just come up."

"Uh, yeah. That would have been less dangerous for me," Ophelia continued rubbing.

"You okay?" Kyle's voice tenuous.

"I'm fine. What do you want?"

"We're all meeting in the library in about thirty minutes. The girls are there already. Amry said she forgot to set the alarm to get you up—she had that early science class."

"So, are you the errand boy?" Ophelia asked, sarcastically.

"No. Well, kind of. I had to go back to my room for something and you were on the way. I volunteered." Kyle turned his gaze to the campus.

"Okay, you've done your job. I'll be there in a few minutes. First, I need to get dressed and put ice on my face." She said as she gave him the finger.

"I deserved that. I'll see you there." Kyle briskly crossed the lawn.

Ophelia went to the bathroom and turned on the shower. She was the only one of her friends who still maintained the morning ritual. She gazed in the mirror while waiting for the water to steam. Squinting her eyes, she leaned in for a better view. Yup, a knot the size of a nickel angrily sat between her eyes. Ugh, why today? A haze of hot mist blurred her reflection and indicated it was time to get in. Standing under the rain of comfort, her body relaxed as she soaked in the peace. She had a feeling this would be the only quiet for a while.

Life at the Academy was about to find a whole new meaning.

———

Ophelia rounded the corner of the library and slid through the honey oak doors. Her friends were seated at one of the many rectangular tables in the center of the building. Surrounded on all four sides by books dating back to the twelfth century, Ophelia stood for a moment taking in the aroma. It tickled her nostrils and surrounded her mind with exhilaration. She was the sponge to the waterfall of knowledge contained in this room, its sole purpose to deliver pleasure to her waiting senses.

"Over here!" Amry called her. "What are you doing?" she asked smiling.

"Just taking it all in." Ophelia sat down.

"Honestly, you make me laugh. You're in here just about every day of the week and it still excites you."

"Yes, it does. There's so much to learn, and the information is practically endless. Why, don't you feel like that?"

"Well, sure. I like coming here but it doesn't quite affect me the same way. Are you okay today?"

"Sure. Why wouldn't I be?" Ophelia's eyes widened.

"You weren't yourself yesterday. I mean you were, but extra stressed. Sort of mousy. I barely heard you utter a word all day. Was it because we were called into Headmaster's office?"

"No. It wasn't the highlight of my day. You know I hate dealing with adults, but that wasn't it." Ophelia looked away.

"What then?" Amry reached out and patted Ophelia's hand.

"It was my anniversary." Ophelia said in a shaky voice.

"Oh. I'm so sorry. I forgot. No wonder you were a bundle of nerves."

"It's okay. It's over and time to move on." Ophelia gave a slight smile.

"Hey, what happened to your face?' Amry reached out but Ophelia quickly retracted.

"Don't. The damn thing is throbbing. Kyle thought it would be a good idea to throw rocks at my window." Ophelia's eyes narrowed.

"Kyle, you're an idiot." Amry wrinkled her forehead.

"What? It was an accident. I told her I was sorry."

"He did," Bethany chimed in.

"Can we get on with this? Sawyer gets here in twenty minutes." Ophelia glanced at the antique clock on the wall.

"I don't know what to do with this," said Kyle looking uneasy. "I mean we all know the reason why he's coming here which does nothing to support why Headmaster thinks he'll be safe. If Sawyer's father gets wind of where he is, this place is going to become hell and I'm not sure what any of us will be able to do to protect him. It's not like we're confronting a snobby cheerleader. His life will be at risk, but our fate could be much worse."

Silence surrounded the table. They all understood what Kyle meant. There are worse things than death.

Ophelia shuddered. Thoughts of the worse picked at her brain, devouring every ounce of excitement she felt for the day.

"I think he's here." Ophelia pointed at the door.

Freshmen to seniors stopped what they were reading to look up. Most of them had not seen a breather since their transition. The air carried a ribbon of discontent that wrapped itself around the room, squeezing out every drop of pleasure.

Mr. Coal and Mr. Rain sandwiched the male teen, escorting him to the woeful group. Ophelia's heartbeat faster the closer he got; her mood quickly shifting. She intertwined her fingers nervously. Lightly tousled, brown locks framing a firm jaw and intense hazel eyes stole Ophelia's attention. Running her fingertips over the protruding knot, she turned away when they reached the table.

Mr. Rain was the first to speak.

"Sawyer, these are the kids we told you about. They will

show you around the school and help you with whatever you need. Mr. Burkletter will be sharing his dorm room. Feel free to ask him any questions you might have about the curriculum."

"Wait. What? No one said anything about giving up my room." Kyle scowled.

"You're not giving it up, Mr. Burkletter. You are sharing it." Mr. Rain glared at Kyle.

"Whatever. I wasn't told." Kyle shoved his chair back.

"I'm really sorry. Maybe the Headmaster can find me another room." Sawyer's tone was apologetic.

"That won't be necessary. Mr. Burkletter will be happy to make room. Isn't that right?" Mr. Rain squeezed Kyle's shoulder.

"Sure." Kyle rolled his eyes.

"All settled then. Sawyer, we will leave you to get acquainted with your new friends. Your things have been delivered to the dorm and we'll will be around if you need us."

The set of khakis left as awkward as they had entered.

"What a pair of goons," Bethany quipped.

The friends nodded in agreement.

Sawyer's stare made them squirm.

"What the hell are you staring at?" Kyle sighed.

"Nothing. Never mind." Sawyer tightly wrapped his arms over his chest.

"It's okay. You're pretty damn strange to us, too. Come on, sit down." Amry pulled a chair out.

Reluctantly, Sawyer melted down and scooted back, creating a minuscule of distance between them.

"So, your dad, he's after you?" Ophelia joined the conversation.

"Yes. He killed my mom."

"We read that. I'm sorry." Ophelia locked eyes.

"Read it?" Sawyer inquired.

"In your file, the Headmaster had us review."

"Oh, I have a file?"

"You do, I'm sorry."

"For what?" Sawyer relaxed his arms.

"Having a dad like that. The horrible things he's done to your family, I couldn't imagine."

"Yeah. He took my mother, but when he changed, he took my father too. There isn't anything left of the man that used to be my dad."

Sawyer turned his head from right to left, tightening his arms again.

"My turn for a question." He looked directly at Ophelia. "Why are you here?"

"Me?"

"All of you? This place makes no sense." Sawyer knitted his brows. "What's the purpose to the whole thing? Why haven't you, you know?"

"Why haven't we what?" Ophelia was confused.

"The breather is asking why we haven't moved on," Kyle grumbled.

"Oh. I can't answer for everyone, but for myself it's a choice."

"How can you have a choice? That's lunacy."

The others pushed further away from the table. It was them against the breather. Only Ophelia remained close.

"My little sister, Haven, is lost. I stay so I can search for her. When our beginning came, we were separated. She's only seven. I can't go until I find her." Ophelia wiped her eyes.

"No tears." Sawyer stretched his neck to see better.

"What?" Ophelia blinked.

"You wiped your eyes as if there were tears. There are none."

"Oh. I know. Sometimes I can still feel them. Trying to wipe them away is just a reflex."

"You said you were separated from your sister when it was your beginning. What does that mean?"

"Enough for now." Kyle stood up. "He doesn't need to know all of our surreptitious history."

"Surrept... what?" Sawyer stood as well.

"Great. He's a breather, dangerous to us, and stupid too," Kyle shouted.

The entire room of students stared at them.

"Sit down the both of you. You, you're a stranger to our group and school. I should think you would be feeling a little more grateful and a lot less judgmental," Amry scolded.

"I wasn't judging. This is so damn confusing. I mean I'm sitting here talking to you, all of you, and you're—dead."

Ophelia hadn't heard those words in over a hundred years. Like a knife, they pierced through her ghostly shell and ripped open the cavity where her heart would be. It had been so long since she had seen her family. Her mother and father must have been inconsolable the day she and Haven started their beginning.

It was spring, her favorite season. The trees were growing fat with new, lush green leaves. Flowers bloomed the most brilliant hues of pink, purple and yellow. The air had transcended from a morning chill to an eight in the morning toast and tea on the sun-drenched porch. Her mother had asked if she would watch Haven for a few hours while both parents did some shopping in town. The following week her little sister would turn eight, and they wanted to surprise her. They were picking up a brand-new dollhouse that her father had ordered from England.

Ophelia didn't mind. She liked spending time with her. As siblings went, they were close. Maybe it was the large span of years between them, but Ophelia felt more like an aunt than a big sister. Whatever the reason, it was fine with her.

Their parents had been gone about an hour and Haven was playing in the front yard. Ophelia had nestled into a rocker on the porch and was reading one of her favorite books, Molly Make-Believe by Eleanor Hallowell Abbott. Rarely did a motor car come down their street but they had been instructed by their father to stay away when it did. Ophelia set her book on a side table when she heard the honking of a horn in the distance. Standing to see which direction it was coming from, she noticed Haven running out into the street to retrieve a ball that had gotten away.

Ophelia bolted down the eight steps and across the lawn in time to see the car coming from the right and her sister facing the other way. Without a thought, she ran into the middle of the road and wrapped her arms around Haven before hearing a dissonant thud. When she woke up, her sister was running toward a man standing at the end of their block. She screamed for her to come back, but it was too late. He and Haven were gone.

Through the years she was able to find out that the man is a soul gatherer. He takes the newly deceased when their spirits are confused and lures them with hope. He especially likes the innocence of children. No one is sure where he keeps them, but a few have been able to escape. Most of them adults. Once they leave, all their knowledge of his location fades away. Perhaps he is able to cast a powerful spell, none of them ever have answers. What they can remember is he's not cruel, but lonely. Ophelia surmised he must be lost himself. Protectors, like Mr. Coal and Mr. Rain, have tried through the years to find his hidden sanctuary but each time they get close, he manages to cloak his secret once again.

The light has come for her several times over the past one hundred and seven years, and it will keep coming until she finds Haven.

"It's called the beginning because that is when you start your forever. Before that we are on earth for a few years living a mortal life. After we die, that's when the real living begins. The state of being that lasts always. Yesterday was my anniversary."

"Anniversary? Of your death?" Sawyer's voice screeched.

"Yes," Ophelia spoke, softly.

"I feel nauseous." Sawyer rubbed his gut.

This time Bethany jumped into the conversation. A rarity, she preferred listening to participating.

"Let me get this straight, your father, a demon hunter, turned to the dark side and killed your mother. Now he wants to kill you, too, so he can get brownie points with the underworld. And you're blown away because we're all spirits? Really?" Bethany smirked.

"How did you know all that about me?" Sawyer asked.

All four teens in unison spoke.

"The file."

"Oh yeah. I forgot about that. What was in this file?"

"We know your uncle Dillon is the one who saved you and brought you here. He's your mom's brother?"

"Yup. I miss him so much right now." Sawyer slouched down further in his seat.

Sawyer's expression was a road map for sadness and defeat.

"Listen, I know this is all too much at one time. You feel strange, we feel strange too. Most of these kids haven't seen a breather in decades. You're a reminder of the life they once had. But we're gonna have to all make it work to keep you, and us, safe." Ophelia reached for his hand, but Sawyer pulled back.

"Keep you safe? You're dead. What more could happen?'

"Mr. Abernathy, the Headmaster, started this school for kids who were stuck in limbo. I'm one of the exceptions because I choose to stay." Ophelia looked to the distance. "He wanted to make a place for them that would be safe while they wait for the light. Most of the time it happens within the four years of high school. But, if it doesn't, those souls get to stay on and help run the school."

Ophelia's gaze traveled from Sawyer to the group. "However, there is a place that no one likes to talk about. A place where a soul can be lost forever." Ophelia quivered.

"Like hell?"

"You could call it that. But it's not like what you were taught in Sunday school. There's no fire and brimstone. The soul is surrounded by an unending tunnel of darkness. Imagine being lost out in space forever. No one to talk to, nothing to see, just the bitter cold of night for eternity."

Sawyer drew his knees up close to his chest, clasped them and buried his head in his forearms.

"I'm sorry to put you all at risk. How could this happen to you?"

"Someone very powerful and filled with darkness can possess the ability. Someone like your father."

Sawyer looked up at them, tears streaming down his cheeks. He wiped them away with his sleeve. Ophelia reached out once again, this time he didn't pull away.

"I can touch you. You're cold." He half-smiled.

"We can manipulate our energy to feel solid but not all the time. It's too draining."

Ophelia gazed over at her three friends. They appeared to be softening, even Kyle. She took the opportunity to use everyone's vulnerability for the greater good.

"Sawyer, we can watch out for you, be your friend and help you, but you're gonna have to trust us, too. Now that you know you're not the only one at risk, maybe we can help each other. The rest of the school will be curious but if you stick with us, things should be okay. Does everyone agree?"

"I know I came on strong man, but the weirdness definitely goes both ways." Kyle scooted in.

"Man? What, did you die in the seventies?" Sawyer chortled.

"Yeah. I did."

"Oh, I'm sorry. I didn't mean anything, I didn't know." Sawyer's smile quickly faded.

"Nah. It's all good. Nineteen seventy-eight, hit by a drunk driver."

Sawyer placed his elbows on the table and then clasping his hands, rested his chin between his two thumbs.

"I guess I'll have to get used to that."

"I guess you will. And we'll have to get used to hearing you breathe," Kyle grinned.

Ophelia gazed at the new living soul, she knew it wasn't possible, the living and the dead couldn't be together. But she had him for a little while.

"Lia, where are you?" Amry snapped her fingers in front of her face.

"Lia? I thought your name was Ophelia?" Sawyer inched closer.

"It is. Lia is what Amry calls me."

"Lia. I like that. Can I call you that too?"

"Sure." Ophelia's core heated. Strange she could feel that.

"Well, I guess I should show you where you're gonna be sleeping tonight." Kyle stood.

"Yeah, we'll all go." Bethany clasped her boyfriend's hand.

The five of them filed out of the library, taking a tour of the campus before ending at Kyle and now, Sawyer's dorm. Plopping on the two beds, their conversation drifted to less paranormal and more... normal. They talked through most of the night and, by the time the sun was peeking out over the horizon, a friendship had bonded them.

3

THE BEGINNING

Over the next several months Sawyer found his place at The Academy of Souls and by the end of his first year, no one paid much attention to the only breather. He had become a part of them. And, although his father had yet to find him, they would be ready when he did.

Ophelia still had her dreams, but that's all they were. The dead cannot love the living without paying a price.

It was three o'clock on a Friday afternoon and everyone was heading over to the Grand Hall. News had spread that two younger students had found their way to the *light*; a celebration in their honor was about to take place. It had been months since Ophelia had heard news about Haven, but she remained hopeful.

Sawyer was coming by her room to pick her up. They had to finalize some details on a project they had in history, and the rest of the group had gone on ahead.

Four rapid knocks on the door. It was Sawyer's code. She hastily straightened out her bed before asking him to come in.

"I brought the last two pages of the report, where do you want them?"

"Oh, here, I'll take them." Ophelia reached out and her hand brushed his.

Sawyer stood frozen, matching her gaze. He moved in closer.

"Lia, I've been wanting to...."

"No don't say it. It's impossible." Ophelia backed up.

"Why?"

"You know why. We have told you how dangerous it could be for you," Ophelia pleaded.

"I don't care." Sawyer moved closer.

"Stop." Ophelia hovered above and floated to the doorway.

In two strides Sawyer was an inch from her body and pulling her close. She let it happen. His lips caressed hers. He was warm, like sunshine on that spring day so many years ago. She knew it was wrong, she knew the danger, but all she could feel was life.

4

THE DREAM

Ophelia shot up from under the warmth of her fluffy, down comforter. She tossed aside the pale, green fabric so abruptly, half of it cascaded down to the floor. Shaky with emotions she did not want, she let her legs slide down to the cherry, wood floor. Clutching her chest, she tried to hold in the yearning burning inside. What was happening to her? She tried to cast off her latest dream, sending it floating into space, far from the inner sanctum of her mind. But it wouldn't, or rather, she couldn't. Sawyer would never come to her room to profess his love.

The boy had enough trouble hiding from his evil, ex-demon hunting father. Throwing a forbidden romance into the mix would surely break him.

He had been living at The Academy for over twelve months now and, the more she tried to ignore the feelings that plagued her every time she looked into his suede hazel eyes—soft and delicate—the pull only deepened. It started the first day he walked into the library with his entourage of goons, Mr. Coal and Mr. Rain, that she had seen his true nature. Yes, his eyes were warm and beautiful, but it was what was behind them that drew her into the torture she now endured each day. His soul. The strength and kindness that lay behind the brightest hues of green, brown, and gold was only the beginning to the boy.

At first, she tossed off the dreams that would visit her late at night, when she lay vulnerable in her bed. If she were like everyone else, sleep would be the smile of a distant memory. But she wasn't.

Ophelia's talents for crossing the bridge between the dead and the living were perplexing but navigating feelings about Sawyer for over a year brought anguish. His way of making her giggle through the sadness of empty leads for Haven, or how she tingled when his hand brushed hers, added layers of confusion and indecision.

Could she be so bold as to profess her feelings? Not an option. And if he felt the same, where could it go anyway?

Opening the window, to the courtyard below, she scanned the students for a familiar face. Amry was sitting at a picnic table reading her favorite genre, a time travel romance called *The Dusk Chronicles*. Ophelia recognized the book from the cover. She quickly showered, dressed, and made it to the courtyard just as Amry was getting up.

"Hey, I wondered when you were gonna wake up. You can really snooze." Amry placed a bookmark on the page and closed it.

"Yeah. I know." Ophelia groaned. "I wish I knew why I still do this. Don't you guys ever get tired?"

"Nope. We're dead. How are we possibly gonna get tired? I think it's a psychological thing." Amry curled her lip.

Amry's father was a child psychologist. She grew up in a house that recognized other kids' problems, just not their own.

"Really? You're gonna pull the psych card on me?" Ophelia frowned.

"Psych card? Wow. You're starting to sound like a real, twentieth century girl." Amry grinned.

"I am a real, twentieth century girl."

"Barely. I don't think the ten years you spent in the beginning of the century had much influence on your current choice of verbiage."

"Oh no?"

"Nope. That's all me." Amry lightly punched Ophelia in the shoulder. "I got to head out. Calculus is about to start, and I can't be late. One more and it's straight to Abernathy's."

"Yeah, I better get going, too. I told Sawyer I'd meet him at the library so we can discuss our American History project."

"Sawyer, huh? Be careful, girlie."

"There's nothing to be careful with." Ophelia turned away.

"You still have the dreams, Lia?"

"Only here and there. It's okay."

"Lia. You know that would be the end of you. Not to mention what could happen to Sawyer," Amry warned.

"I know. I don't need it repeated a hundred times over. Besides, he has no clue. Believe me, we're as safe as it gets."

"Yeah, I'm not so sure about that."

Ophelia watched her friend as she glided through the courtyard and disappeared. She wanted to ask her why she had said that about Sawyer. Had he said something to her? But she didn't. That would only fan a fire that didn't need to be ignited.

The library was on the other side of the campus and gliding would get her there in a snap, but the day glowed with droplets of sunshine on the dew of the new grass, and Ophelia preferred to walk in the beauty. She raised her cheeks towards the warmth and smiled: death's little pleasures.

The time spent with Sawyer at the library was uneventful and strictly business. She had worked hard to keep it that way, on her side anyway. Sawyer never showed much interest in her other than friendship. This made it easier for Ophelia to push her emotions far into the darkness at the edges of her soul. Tucked away, barely a thought, until the dreams. She wished they'd go away. Each night it took longer and longer to fall asleep. Fear of unleashing her inner most desires consumed her quiet time.

She sat back in her chair while Sawyer went to grab some needed books off the shelf. Taking in a deep breath, she slowly exhaled. The library was her place. The home she'd never know again, the people she'd never see again. Everything contained in these four walls reminded her of the life she once had. The full, plush, brown leather chairs in the reading area were like the ones her father put in his study. The smell of lilac from a candle burning on the librarian's desk, carried thoughts of her mother's garden. This was a calm place of reflection.

"I found what we needed." Sawyer's strong voice carried through the air.

"Oh. Great." Ophelia scooted forward.

"We only have a few minutes left before the bell rings; you want to meet here after lunch? I don't have any afternoon classes."

As luck would have it, Ophelia was free in the afternoon too.

"Sure. One o'clock?"

"Yup. I'll see you then."

Sawyer packed up his books in the navy blue backpack he carried every day since he arrived. Ophelia wasn't sure of all of its contents, but she had a feeling something important made a home in the front pouch. Sawyer shied away from anyone else touching it, other than himself.

First period was science. Luckily, it was only two doors away from the library, and Ophelia's favorite class. After sitting down, she searched for her friends. Bethany and Kyle never sat in the same seat. Playing musical chairs seem to tickle them more than the teacher, Mrs. Sanseverino. Mrs. S for short, was a kind, warm-hearted woman. She had been a teacher in life, so it was a natural transition for her at the Academy. And, although patience was a virtue she mastered, Ophelia's friends tested her relentlessly. Today, they were at the back of the class by one of the three large windows that inhabited the west wall.

"Hey, why don't you guys come up here by me?" Ophelia waved to her friends. "There's two seats open."

"Nah. You come back here. We like it by the window, saved you a seat." Kyle pointed to the open chair.

Ophelia was at odds. She wanted to sit by her friends, but she also didn't want to upset Mrs. S. by changing seats.

"Ophelia, come on." Bethany curled her bottom lip.

"Ahem. Go on Miss Wetherton." A voice echoed from the front of the class.

Ophelia whipped her head around and Mrs. S. was seated at her desk. The teacher gestured with a nod of her chin, and a smile, that it was okay for Ophelia to move. Quietly gathering her things, she kept her eyes on the floor and glided to the back. She hated drawing attention to herself, especially when it was from a teacher.

"I dread the way you two tease her every day. Mrs. S. is so sweet, can't you just sit in your assigned seats?" Ophelia furrowed her brow.

"What fun is that?" Kyle smirked.

"Yeah, what fun is that?" Bethany chimed in.

There she goes again, sticking to him like peanut butter on bread. Ophelia chuckled to herself.

"Never mind. Did you see Amry on campus?" Ophelia opened her book to the assigned page.

"Yeah, she said to tell you she'll catch up with you at lunch. There was something she had to do this morning after first period," Kyle said doodling on the cover of his notebook.

"Huh. Okay, thanks."

Ophelia gazed out of the floor to ceiling window to the outside world. The sky was a deep blue with charcoal clouds quickly filling the crevices usually reserved for sunshine. The atmosphere had changed since she'd first glance out of her bedroom window.

She shivered.

"Knock that off," Kyle ordered.

"What did I do?" Ophelia's eyes widened.

"The shivering. It's ridiculous. I swear girl, there's something seriously wrong with you."

"I don't know why it bothers you so much?"

"It's strange. And, I'm not the only one, it really creeps out Sawyer. I mean the guy had to adjust to the dead and here you are flipping the switch. You're not a breather, you're not a total spirit; what are you? I don't blame him." Kyle poked her with his pen.

"Darn." Ophelia rubbed her arm.

"See. Right there, that's what I'm talking about. How the hell did you feel that?"

Ophelia turned her head away from him. She knew it was strange, but she didn't know it frightened Sawyer. Her stomach churned, sending a sour taste to the back of her throat. If she only knew why her ties to the living remained so tightly woven into each other. Life is life, and death is eternal. This shouldn't be happening to her and, yet, here she was engaged in another pointless conversation about the oddities that are, Ophelia Wetherton.

"I'm sorry, Ophelia. You know my mouth and brain don't always work well together." Kyle reached for her hand, but she retracted.

"Did Sawyer really say I scare him?" She looked into Kyle's eyes.

"Uh, no. He's not afraid of you, he just thinks it's weird. But you've said it yourself, it's not ordinary. I didn't mean to hurt you. Can you forgive me?" Kyle pouted.

Ophelia looked up at the ceiling and swiveled around with her back to Kyle. She nodded her head in agreement. It was the only way she could answer him without showing Kyle how his words had pierced her heart. She was used to it from Kyle. He was an idiot at times, but to think Sawyer was...she pushed the thought out of her mind, it was easier.

When lunch rolled around, Ophelia made her way to their usual table. The five of them sort of put stakes down to it when they first came to the Academy. The idea of calling it a lunch break always tickled Ophelia's funny bone. Food was not something any of them did any longer, not even her. They tried calling it the afternoon break, but it never caught on.

She figured the routine of it all comforted most of the students. So, instead of rushing to finish their brown sack lunch, or braving the crowds in a cafeteria line to buy hot food, they used their hour for socializing. It worked out great, until the only breather joined them. Sawyer did need to eat, a problem Headmaster Abernathy had to solve quickly. Using magick to prepare food might draw unwanted attention from the boy's father.

Resolution—the crossover. Certain souls were allowed to cross the bridge between the living and the dead. If you worked for the council, say like Mr. Coal and Mr. Rain, two low level, but skilled sorcerers, then you could partake in that liberty. Headmaster would give them a weekly shopping list and it was their job to go on a scavenger hunt. Luckily, they knew exactly where to gather all the supplies needed, the after hours at a nearby Italian deli. It wasn't hot meals, but it was better than nothing.

"I would kill for a hamburger. Well done, with pepper jack cheese and a side of fries." Sawyer pulled salami off the hard roll on his plate.

"I know. It's rough, but it's not forever. Eventually, they'll find your dad and lock him up. Then you can go home." Ophelia gently smiled.

"I hope sooner rather than later. You guys are great, but I miss doing normal things. Sorry, that didn't come out right."

"No. I get it. We all do. You're still part of the world we left behind. Of course you'd miss it." Ophelia tried to sound positive for Sawyer but, inside, her heart ached.

"Hey. Whatcha guys talking about?" Amry sat down and flipped back her hair.

Ophelia loved to watch her friend's long locks float in gentle waves every time she did that.

"My yearning for grilled meat." Sawyer winced at his sandwich.

"Still missing that burger and fries, huh?" Amry rested her chin on her fists.

"Yup. Every day."

"Where were you this morning? Kyle said you had something to do?" Ophelia questioned.

"I did. But I don't want to say anything until I'm sure. Trust me?" Amry grinned.

"Yes, of course."

"Great. As soon as I have all I need, I'll let you know. Promise."

"Let her know what?" Kyle scooted in to sit next to Amry.

"What I was doing this morning." Amry replied.

"Ohhhh, is it a secret?" said Kyle, rubbing his hands together.

"Sort of, for now." Amry rubbed Ophelia's hand.

"Lia, I promise you'll be the first to know when I figure this out. Kyle, back off." Amry demanded.

"Why are you telling him to back off, what did he do?" Bethany plopped down next to her boyfriend.

"Nothing. Everyone, just never mind where I was this morning. You will all know when the time is right. Which is not now." Amry huffed.

"Easy," Sawyer said, softly. "Whatever it is, you'll tell us when you're ready. Now, enough of that. I got a question. How do we start a bonfire? I'm throwing this sandwich right into the flames."

5

THE SECRET

The sunset projected a kaleidoscope of orange, gold, and a hint of pink across the western hemisphere. Ophelia gasped at the beauty. She never grew tired of it. Spending most of the afternoon with Sawyer only intensified her happiness. The sunset was a mere cherry on the cake.

It was Friday night, weekend fun with her friends. The five of them planned a night at the movie theater. That was Ophelia's favorite place. While the group hunkered down in the seats, she floated on a pocket of air in the center row, eye level with the screen and submerging herself in the characters and soaking up every bit of dialogue. She had only seen one movie before that car took her future, and it was only a short black and white documentary on the blizzards in New York City.

This was so much more. She was completely enamored with anything Hollywood. Ophelia swore that if her life hadn't been taken so abruptly, she would have been an actress like Mary Pickford. She wasn't much bigger than the actress, who knows, maybe she would have been America's darling.

Sawyer had told her once, for him, it was a taste of home. Before his dad turned, and his mom was alive, they were a happy family. Their big night out was pizza and a movie but, when the demon hunter became the demon, that life was shattered. This was a sliver of what was. Ophelia felt sorry for him. Yes, her life had been cut short, and Haven's too. Her beautiful little sister. But to live knowing your father killed your mother was beyond any horror of the instantaneous death that befell her.

Ophelia peered down at her friends who were lined up in the middle row directly underneath her. Amry had waved for her to come down, but Ophelia just nodded. She was where she wanted to be. The film was a comedy from the late nineties, Galaxy Quest. A favorite of Sawyer's, Ophelia enjoyed it but preferred silent films.

Lying back, her body glided on the tracks of air, swaying her slightly. The opulent decor that surrounded her cushioned the part of life that she missed. Her soul soaked in the majesty of a world that had passed her by. The stories she watched on-screen were nothing like the time she knew. Modern, contemporary, urban, these words gnawed at her. That was Sawyer's world. She glanced down at him, his eyes tearing from laughter. Shaking it off, she pulled herself back to the present.

Ophelia hadn't noticed when the stranger that was seated next to Amry arrived. They were engaged in conversation. He was an older gentleman wearing a black suit, white shirt, with a long gray beard draping over the collar and nestling on his round belly. An Amish style hat hid most of his face. He leaned in close, and they were whispering. Abruptly, they ended their talk, and he left.

"Lia. Can you come down here for a sec?" Amry called.

Ophelia sat up and floated down to an empty seat next to her.

"Everything alright?" Ophelia whispered.

"Yeah. I had a question for you. When Haven ran out into the street to get the ball, where were you?"

"What? Why are you asking me this? You know where I was." Ophelia curled her bottom lip.

"The porch, right?"

"Yes."

"You heard the horn, saw the car and ran out to Haven, right?"

"That is correct but why are you bringing this up?" Ophelia pleaded.

"I need to be sure I got the facts right," Amry replied.

"The facts? Please Amry, tell me what is going on."

"Will you two take it outside, we're trying to watch the movie," Kyle scolded.

"Okay Lia, let's go to the lobby."

The two girls whisked toward the lobby. Ophelia sat down on the bottom step of the staircase that led to the balcony.

"Amry. I don't know what you're doing but stop. You, of all people, know how badly this upsets me. I haven't heard any new information about the soul gatherer or Haven in months. Bringing up that day just makes it worse," Ophelia pleaded.

"I'm sorry, Lia. I know it's painful. But I was trying to help you."

"Help me, how? And who was that man you were talking to?"

"Albert Johnson, he helps lost souls. I tracked him down after overhearing a conversation from some of the teachers.

Amry sat down next to Ophelia.

"And what was it you wanted from him?"

"Two things, actually. First, to find out if he knew anything on Haven and the soul gatherer."

Ophelia eyes widened. "Does he?"

"He's gonna work on it. Says he knows who we're talking about. The soul gatherer has been around a long time, way before Mr. Johnson got here. He has a contact he can speak to. He'll get back to us in a few days." Amry rubbed Ophelia's shoulder.

"And the second thing?"

"Um, that's one I wanted to find out for you, but also for all of us." Amry wriggled.

"Just say it. You're making my stomach ball up in knots." Ophelia rubbed her belly.

"That."

"That what?"

"The thing you just did. Rubbing your stomach like it hurts."

"It does hurt." Ophelia knitted her brow.

"I know. But why does it hurt?"

"I just told you."

"No. Why do you feel pain? Warmth? The need to sleep? None of us have experienced anything other than the energy drainage from making ourselves solid for too long. Why, can you do this? I know it bugs you and it confuses us.

"I thought it was time we got some solid answers. Headmaster Abernathy continues to brush it off. Tells us he'll look into it, but I think he already knows and doesn't want to say. That's why I asked Mr. Johnson to help. But I wanted to be sure the facts I gave him were correct." Amry leaned into Ophelia.

"You know they are," Ophelia spoke in a small voice.

"I do. But this had to be accurate so we could get answers. I was just fact checking. Hey, I thought you'd be excited?"

"I am. It's just, I don't know if I want to hear the answer. What if it's something creepy?"

"Something creepy?" Amry laughed. "We're already dead, how much creepier can we get?"

Ophelia heartily laughed. All the tension she felt a moment ago, vanished. Amry was right. No matter what the explanation, did it really matter? She is celestial, no coming back from that. A surge of electricity raced through her pseudo veins once she allowed the thought to take hold. Maybe she would finally find out why she is different. And Haven...

"He told me the soul gatherer has been here since forever. Like the beginning. No one knows what happened to him and why he won't cross. But he's fondest of the children. Maybe something happened to his own kids or something. I don't know. Hopefully, Mr. Johnson will be able to help you find Haven."

"I miss her so much. The thought that she's out there alone, sickens me. Our parents don't know what happened to us." Ophelia lay her head in her lap.

"Especially if they crossed over. It's difficult to come back once you take the light. Nearly impossible." Amry frowned.

"They would have crossed thinking they would see us. If I can find Haven, we can be united." Ophelia lifted her head and smiled.

"I know. It will be a happy and sad day," said Amry, looking away.

"What's wrong?" Ophelia was confused.

"You'll be gone. I'll be alone."

"No you won't. You'll still have Kyle and Bethany. Besides, maybe if I'm gone, you'll figure out why you're still here. Then we can be together on the other side. You'll see your family again, too."

Ophelia tried to soothe her friend. It hurt her too. The thought of never seeing Amry again tore her up. If it weren't for her, Ophelia would have gone down a dark path right after she got to the Academy. She had blamed herself for losing Haven to the soul gatherer. It was Amry who brought her back.

"You're right. The whole thing is so weird though. You'd think after all these years, I'd get used to the whole dead thing. But the truth is, most of the time I'm clueless. I just put up a good front. I do miss my family, but I've never spent too much time on the why. I just knew I was here." Amry's voice quivered.

Ophelia reached for her friend's hand and intertwined their fingers.

"We'll figure this out. Thank you, for trying to find Haven. And also, for me. I wish I knew you when I was alive."

The two girls hugged, and Ophelia squeezed a little tighter before letting go.

"Yeah, me too. Although, by the time I was born, you'd been dead for a really, long time." Amry grinned.

"Details." Ophelia smiled. "So, where do we go from here?"

"We wait. Mr. Johnson said he should know something in a few days."

Ophelia returned back to her comfort spot, and let the movie shove out all the questions. There would be plenty of those over the next few days. For now, she needed to laugh.

6

THE IN-BETWEEN

Two days had passed since Amry had told her about Mr. Johnson and the quest to find Haven and Ophelia's oddity with the living. The waiting was the worst, and no matter how many questions she had for Amry, there were no answers yet.

It was Sunday evening and there were no Monday classes. The teachers were off to a yearly council meeting to discuss the curriculum for the new year. Or, at least that's what they told the students. Ophelia felt there was more to it, but there was no evidence of this assumption--only her gut interfering with her brain. She decided to settle in and read a new book, 77 *Shadow Street* by Dean Koontz. He had become her favorite author in death. The books had drastically changed over the past one hundred eight years, and she for one, loved it.

A trickle of chills ran up her spine and her hands ached from the night air. Closing the window, she decided a hot shower would melt away the beginning of spring which, in the evening, offered a complete contrast to the seventy plus degrees of the day. Apparently, she wasn't the only one to feel the angst of the living. Someone needed to tell the Academy it operated in the world of the dead and stop with the seasonal changes.

Wrapped in a plush, pale pink robe, she pulled the comforter down on her bed and wriggled underneath the covers. Fluffing her pillow, she propped it up against the wall and enjoyed the moment.

Closing her eyes, Ophelia could almost picture her bedroom in the house she had loved so much. A large oak dresser with an oak trimmed mirror that hung on the wall struck the eye as you walked into her room. Her mother had a large, paisley patterned, area rug placed under her four-poster bed for the cold winter mornings. A gold, brocade comforter with tiny, brown flowers was the main attraction. It had been ordered from Europe and took several months to arrive. Ophelia adored the lush, plump feeling as it draped over her at night.

Opening her eyes, she squirmed further down, tucking the comforter under her chin. Inhaling the scent of print to paper, she turned the page to the first chapter.

Bam! Bam! The deep knocking resonated throughout her room. Startled, Ophelia shot up, dropping her book on the floor.

"Lia!" Amry's voice was penetrating.

"Coming. Give me a second."

Ophelia sliced through air to save time, she was at the door and unlocking in the blink of an eye.

"You need to get dressed. Now." Amry started pulling clothes out from Ophelia's side of the closet.

"What's wrong? You're scaring me." Ophelia slid into her jeans and snatched the sweater from Amry's hand.

"You should be. We all are. Sawyer's demon-loving father has been spotted in town."

"So? Town is in the corporeal world, why should we be worried?" Ophelia picked up her book and tossed it on the bed.

"Because, if he's in town, he's only a few miles away from us. If he figures out how to pass through the portal, then we're all dead."

"What about Mr. Rain and Mr. Coal? They can protect us. And Dictator Dick, isn't that his job?"

"Do you really think some low-level sorcerers and a pumped-up security guard are going to be able to stop an ex-demon hunter who's gone completely out of his mind? The man wants to kill his own son, not to mention the fact he killed Sawyer's mother. We are screwed if he finds out how to get here." Amry grabbed Ophelia's arm. "Let's go.

"Where are we going?"

"Kyle and Bethany are waiting for us downstairs. Head-master wants us to take Sawyer and hide in the *in-between*."

"The in-be...what?" Ophelia's eyes widened.

"I'll explain on the way. Let's go, now!"

The two girls didn't bother with any conventional means of travel, one step through the wall and they were in the lobby with Kyle and Bethany.

"Where's Sawyer?" Ophelia spun around searching the room.

"He's in the Headmaster's office. We're going there now." Amry cupped Ophelia's hand.

Two steps forward placed them in the office of Headmaster Abernathy. Sawyer was standing in the middle of the room surrounded by the *khaki twins*, Mr. Coal and Mr. Rain, Dictator Dick, and Abernathy himself.

"All of you, hurry up," the Headmaster insisted.

Sawyer's face had lost all color, his lower lip quivered when he laid eyes on them. His fear filled the room, drawing each one of them closer to console him. Ophelia's heart cavity mimicked a frenetic pounding as if the organ still lay nestled in her chest. She clenched her fist to her breastbone to quiet the sound filling her ears.

"Miss Wetherton, are you alright?" Dictator Dick gave her disapproving glare.

"I'm fine. Don't worry about me," Ophelia snapped. She hated his tone.

"I need the four of you to take Mr. Sawyer to the *in-between* and stay there until you get word from me that it's alright to come back." Abernathy hustled them all into a circle.

"What if we don't hear from you?" Kyle asked.

"If it's not one of us present in this room, then flee. Take Mr. Sawyer to a destination you feel will be safe and tell no one."

"How long should we wait?"

"Give us the day. If he has not uncovered any new information, I think the demon hunter will be on his way. He's moving about in the living world, no one there will be able to help him. If we remain diligent here, and keep the portal closed, all should be fine."

"And the students here? What if he gets through?" Ophelia frowned.

"Let me worry about that. Now all of you join hands, tightly. We don't want one of you winding up in another realm."

Ophelia clasped Amry on her left and Sawyer on her right. The others reached for the person next to them. They had formed a tightly woven circle.

"I don't understand. Where are we going? What is the *in-between?*" Ophelia's eyes widened.

"Miss Wetherton, we don't have time for this. You will see soon enough."

Abernathy raised his hands and commanded six words. "Not here, not there, not anywhere."

Sawyer gasped as the blackness creeped down the walls of the room, cloaking them in the darkness. Ophelia squeezed his hand tightly and he returned the gesture. Amry whispered words of comfort in her ear, but they did little to ease her apprehension. The Headmaster's voice grew further and further away as the blackness coddled their bodies and lifted them, weightless in the atmosphere.

Ophelia shut her eyes. The movement made her dizzy. She pushed back the churning nausea with her throat muscles, holding the sour taste of bile at bay. She hoped Amry would hear from Mr. Johnson when they got back. *If* they got back. The idea of tasting and feeling something that has been gone over hundred years was beginning to freak her out. A hot shower was one thing, but phantom organs giving real sensation—she needed answers.

"Lia, open your eyes. We're here."

Ophelia tapped her foot on solid ground and sighed.

"Come on you, open them." Amry laughed.

Ophelia opened her eyes. On her left she clearly saw The Academy, and to her right, the little town where the living held residence.

"This is so weird." She reached her hand to the school, the image blurred.

"What the heck is this?" Sawyer's voice trembled.

"We are kind of in nowhere. The two worlds surround us and we're occupying the space that separates them. Sort of like a doorway. On one side, your room, on the other, the dorm hallway. We're standing directly in the doorway." Amry grinned.

"Why the hell are you grinning? This is not funny." Sawyer exclaimed.

"I think it's kind of funny," Amry replied. "We can see everything that is going on in both places, but they have no clue we're watching them. Oh crap. Uh, look over there, isn't that your dad?" Amry extended a shaky arm.

Sawyer's eyes widened as his chin dropped toward his chest. "No, no, no, no." Backing up, he shook his head repeatedly from side to side. Pushing down a gulp he forced out his response.

"That's him. The bastard that tore my mom to pieces." Sawyer swiped the pooling water from his eyes. "But, he's not my dad. That man died the day he turned. This is a monster." Sawyer raised his fist to the invisible shield.

"Don't." Kyle grabbed Sawyer's shirt and pulled him back. "If you disrupt the landscape, you'll tear a hole in that world. Your dad will find us."

"So, what? We just stand here?" Sawyer's voice deepened.

"You can walk along the path of blackness, you can sit down, and you can lay down, but don't disrupt the wall that separates us. And don't wander too far. You wouldn't want to happen on another dimension and then, poof, you're gone."

Sawyer crossed his legs and collapsed down, facing the town and his maniacal father. Ophelia sat next to him, and he scooted closer, touching his knee to hers. The others took the cue and sat too.

Ophelia stretched her neck to get a better look at the demon hunter without breaking her contact with Sawyer. She winced when she had a clear view of the man's face. Yellow eyes and flared nostrils bore the hate he felt. It saddened her to see his passion for the blood of his own son.

"You said once it was your mother that made him snap. What did she do?" She turned to Sawyer.

"He thought she had fallen in love with my uncle, but it wasn't true. I guess all those years hunting evil caught up with him. He refused to believe her. My uncle tried to help but my dad thought that he was protecting her." Sawyer clasped his hands behind his head. "He thought my uncle, his brother, was in love with my mom. Truth was, my uncle was just trying to save my family, *including* his brother."

Sawyer pulled away from Ophelia and abruptly stood up. She sighed to herself.

"My dad wants to kill me because he thinks my uncle is really my father. He's all twisted up inside."

Ophelia tried to soothe him. "I'm so sorry this is happening to you."

"Yeah, dude. That is the worst," Kyle chimed in.

Bethany and Amry nodded in agreement.

"Hey, look you guys. He's leaving." Kyle pointed to the demon hunter. The tall, husky figure strutted to a large, black SUV. Opening the car door, he took one last look around the perimeter and got in.

Ophelia watched as Sawyer's monster drove out of town. Her heart ached for the pain her friend was in. She could only imagine what he was feeling.

The vision of town blurred into the blackness, filling the crevices of open space. Swaying with weightlessness once again, Ophelia grasped her stomach. In a moment they were back in the Headmaster's office.

"Children, he's gone." Abernathy cleared his throat.

"We know. We saw him," Sawyer remarked.

"Mr. Sawyer, you did well for occupying the *in-between* for twelve hours. I knew your friends would be fine, but that long in the abyss can do things to the living." Abernathy tilted his head and nodded.

"Twelve hours? It felt like minutes." Sawyer remarked.

"Everyone's okay, I assume?" Dictator Dick interrupted.

"We're fine. That's the weirdest place ever," Sawyer answered.

"Hmm. You've never been to the edge of nowhere," Mr. Coal replied.

"Nope. Can't say that I have, and can say I don't want to go," Sawyer said, sarcastically.

"Well, no worries for now. You were all superb. Thank you, students, for being such a good friend to Mr. Thomas. I'm sure this would be much harder for him without you." Abernathy glared at Sawyer.

"Oh. Yeah, yes. Thanks for sticking with me. I couldn't do this alone. Headmaster, do you think he'll come back?"

"If he gets frustrated enough, yes, I do. But we'll tackle that when it happens, just like we did today. You're safe for now. Why don't you all go back to your rooms? You must be tired."

Abernathy pointed toward the door. They all took the cue and decided to walk back to the dormitories, agreeing there was enough ghostly travel for one day.

Later that evening, Ophelia lay her head down on the over-stuffed pillow she loved so much. Rolling on her side, she grabbed the cushion and cradled it over her head. The visions of the *in-between* gripped her memory and filled up her mind, pushing out all other thoughts. What if Haven was stuck in the *in-between* somewhere? Maybe that's why no one has ever been able to find the soul gatherer. Her last thought before surrendering to the quiet peace of sleep was, *help me Mr. Johnson, please.*

ACKNOWLEDGMENTS

To all my family and friends who consistently show support and encouragement, this journey is nothing without you by my side. Thank you...

Thank you OLV for introducing me to writing and igniting the torch that still burns today.

OPHELIA NEEDS YOUR HELP

Did you enjoy *Ophelia*?
Remember, reviews keep books alive . . .

Alex still needs your help by leaving your review on either
GoodReads or the digital storefront of your choosing.

ABOUT THE AUTHOR

Originally from New York, I currently reside in Nevada. Writing Young Adult paranormal, I find inspiration from events that have been in my life for as long as I can remember. Inheriting the sensitivity to the supernatural from my family, they continue to be an endless source of vision.

I am one of the 2017 & 2018 winners of, 50 Great Writers You Should Be Reading. Most recently, Alex McKenna & The Geranium Deaths received the Gold in the Readers Favorite Book Awards Contest for Young Adult Paranormal.

www.ingramcontent.com/pod-product-compliance
Lightning Source LLC
Chambersburg PA
CBHW070650130626
46555CB00006B/2800